DINGING DOORBELLS

Tameka Fryer Brown

illustrated by

Ebony Glenn

Kokila

At the first dinging doorbell
this holiday I see . . .

a sweet potato pie just for me!

At the second dinging doorbell
this holiday I see:
two selfie queens

and a sweet potato pie just for me.

At the third dinging doorbell
this holiday I see:
three posh sibs,

two selfie queens
and a sweet potato pie just for me.

At the fourth dinging doorbell
this holiday I see:
four pounds of chitlins,

three posh sibs,

two selfie queens

and a sweet potato pie just for me.

At the **fifth** dinging doorbell
this holiday I see:

BAKED MACARONI AND CHEEEEEESE!

Four pounds of chitlins,
three posh sibs,
two selfie queens
and a sweet potato pie just for me.

At the sixth dinging doorbell
this holiday I see:
six toddlers squealing,

BAKED MACARONI AND CHEEEEEESE . . .
four pounds of chitlins,
three posh sibs,
two selfie queens
and a sweet potato pie just for me.

At the seventh dinging doorbell
this holiday I see:
seven brothers repping,

six toddlers squealing,
BAKED MACARONI
            AND CHEEEEEESE . . .
four pounds of chitlins,
three posh sibs,
two selfie queens
and a sweet potato pie just for me.

At the eighth dinging doorbell
this holiday I see:
eight players yelling,

seven brothers repping,

six toddlers squealing,

BAKED MACARONI AND CHEEEEEESE . . .

four pounds of chitlins,

three posh sibs,

two selfie queens

and a sweet potato pie just for me.

At the ninth dinging doorbell
this holiday I see:
nine women whisp'ring,
eight players yelling,
seven brothers repping,
six toddlers squealing,
MORE
MACARONI
AND CHEEEEEESE . . .
four pounds of chitlins,
three posh sibs,
two selfie queens
and a sweet potato pie just for me.

At the tenth dinging doorbell
this holiday I see:
ten dancers sliding,
nine women whisp'ring,
eight players yelling,
seven brothers repping,
six toddlers squealing,
LOTS OF MACARONI AND CHEEEEESE . . .

four pounds of chitlins,
three posh sibs,
two selfie queens
and a sweet potato pie just for me.

At the eleventh dinging doorbell
this holiday I see:
eleven sides a-steaming,
ten dancers sliding,
nine women whisp'ring,
eight players yelling,
seven brothers repping,
six toddlers squealing—
"WHERE'S MY MACARONI AND CHEEEEEESE?"
four pounds of chitlins,
three posh sibs,
two selfie queens
and a sweet potato pie . . .

. . . that was for me.

At the twelfth dinging doorbell
my eyes can hardly see:

twelve crowded steps,
eleven stinky sides,
ten clumsy dancers,
nine nosy women,
eight bad sports,
seven goofy men,
six screeching babies,
WHO NEEDS MACARONI AND CHEEEEESE????
four pounds of yuck,
three bougie snobs,
two silly teens . . .

. . . and a sweet potato pie.
Just for me.